MRS. PELOKI'S SUBSTITUTE

Story by Joanne Oppenheim
Pictures by Joyce Audy Zarins

DODD, MEAD & COMPANY
New York

To Bill —J. O.

To my uncle, Gerard E. Audy —J.A.Z.

Text copyright © 1987 by Joanne Oppenheim
Illustrations copyright © 1987 by Joyce Audy Zarins
All rights reserved
No part of this book may be reproduced in any form
without permission in writing from the publisher
Distributed in Canada by
McClelland and Stewart Limited, Toronto
Printed in Hong Kong by South China Printing Company

1 2 3 4 5 6 7 8 9 10

Library of Congress Cataloging-in-Publication Data

Oppenheim, Joanne.
  Mrs. Peloki's substitute.

  Summary: Mrs. Peloki's substitute experiences the
second grade class at its most difficult.
  [1. Schools—Fiction.   2. Substitute teachers—
Fiction] I. Zarins, Joyce Audy, ill. II. Title.
PZ7.0616Ms 1987 [E] 86-16705
ISBN 0-396-08918-6

On Friday, Mrs. Peloki was writing on the blackboard as
her second graders came back from the lunchroom.

"Why's she wearing her hat and coat?" Marlon whispered to Billy.

"Maybe she's cold," Billy guessed.

"Ahhh-choo!" Mrs. Peloki sneezed. "Ahhh-choo!" She
sneezed again as the door to the classroom opened.

"Who's that?" asked MariEllen.

"A substitute," Marlon groaned.

"I hate substitutes," whispered Wendy.

"Ahhh-choo!" Mrs. Peloki sneezed as she pointed to the words on the blackboard. They said:

"I have a bad cold. I've lost my voice. I must go home. Mrs. Whitey will be here for the rest of the day."

I have a bad cold. I've lost my voice.
I must go home. Mrs. Whitey will
be here for the rest of the day.

Be good helpers!

Mrs. Peloki gave Mrs. Whitey her big brown lesson plan book, some papers, and the keys.

Then Mrs. Peloki wrote three more words on the board.

"Be good helpers!"

"Okey-dokey, Mrs. Peloki!" James started it and pretty soon everyone was saying it as Mrs. Peloki waved good-bye.

"Let's see now." Mrs. Whitey studied the lesson plan book and said, "According to this, we have gym today after…"

"All right!" Marlon cheered.

"Let's go!" hollered Danny.

"Sneakers!" Billy yelled.

There was a stampede to the closet.

"Wait a minute!" said Mrs. Whitey.

"We have to put our sneakers on," said MariEllen, "so we'll be ready for gym."

"Mrs. Peloki lets us," said Stephie.

"That's mine!" Marlon pulled a sneaker out of Danny's hand.

"Give it back," said Danny.

"Ouch!" Wendy cried.

"Boys and girls!" Mrs. Whitey tried to get their attention.

"Stop pushing!" Kevin told Billy.

"I can't find my other sneaker," Stephie complained.

"Here it is. Billy took it," Danny yelled.

Suddenly Mrs. Whitey said firmly, "Freeze! Everybody freeze!"

Everyone froze like statues of ice.

"Good," said Mrs. Whitey. "Now you may melt your feet and go back to your seats."

"But, Mrs. Whi…" Danny began.

"Your lips are frozen tight," said Mrs. Whitey.

With their arms and legs stiff as ice, they slowly clumped back to their desks.

"What are you waiting for?" Mrs. Whitey asked James, who was standing next to his desk.

"I'm stuck," James whispered.

"Stuck?" asked Mrs. Whitey.

"I can't bend my knees. They're frozen."

"Melt," sighed Mrs. Whitey.

James fell like a puddle and everyone laughed.

Everyone except Mrs. Whitey. "That will do," she said firmly. "We've had enough silliness. Gym is at the end of the day. Before we go to gym, we have work to do."

"We're supposed to have show-and-tell," said Danny. "Mrs. Peloki said so. I brought something."

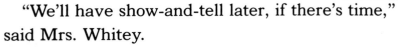

"We'll have show-and-tell later, if there's time,"
said Mrs. Whitey.

"Now take out your pencils and paper for your spelling test."

"Spelling test?" groaned Wendy. "I forgot all about it."

"You're not the only one," whispered Danny.

"I don't have any paper," said Billy.

"Me neither," said MariEllen.

"We use school paper for tests," Stephie told Mrs. Whitey.

"Can I hand it out?" begged Angie.

"No fair," yelled Wendy. "I'm the paper monitor. It says so on the chart."

"Let's settle down," said Mrs. Whitey as she handed Wendy the paper.

"I have to sharpen my pencil," said Angie as she
ran to the sharpener.

"I don't have any pencil," pouted Marlon.

"Me neither," said Danny. "I forgot it. I had to
bring my show-and-tell."

"Never mind," Mrs. Whitey said as she handed them pencils
from Mrs. Peloki's desk. "Please fold your papers in half
and write your name and the date at the top."

"Listen carefully." Mrs. Whitey opened the spelling book. "The first word is *easy*."

"I hope so!" said Billy.

"Yeah, make 'em all simple!" said James.

"Let's stop the talking," said Mrs. Whitey. "Your second word is…"

"Second?" Marlon said. "What was the first?"

"I don't know," shrugged Danny.

"Easy," whispered Stephie. "Number one is *easy*."

"I'm waiting," said Mrs. Whitey.

"Shush!" whispered Wendy.

Billy raised his hand, but Mrs. Whitey ignored him.

"Now, I hope you're all ready. The first word was *easy*. Number two is *not*."

"Not what?" mumbled Angie.

"*Not*," said Mrs. Whitey. "Do not talk. *Not*."

Billy kept waving his hand.

"What is the problem?" asked Mrs. Whitey.

"Look!" Billy said. "Look at Danny's show-and-tell. It's moving!"

"Never mind show-and-tell," said Mrs. Whitey. "We have a spelling test."

"Mrs. Whitey." Marlon stood up. "I got to go to the boys' room."

"Now?" Mrs. Whitey looked at the clock. "We're wasting too much time."

"Can't wait," Marlon called. "Emergency!"

"Marlon always says that," Stephie explained.

"Can I go to the girls' room?" asked MariEllen.

"Oh, well," sighed Mrs. Whitey. "Hurry, please."

"Mrs. Pelo...I mean..." Kevin started coughing and waving his hand.

"What's the trouble, James?" asked Mrs. Whitey.

"I'm Kevin." He coughed some more. "I need a drink."

"Go ahead," Mrs. Whitey said.

"Can I get one, too?" asked Angie. She started coughing.
"Mrs. Whitey, I think my show-and-tell needs a drink,"
said Danny. "Can I get it some water?"

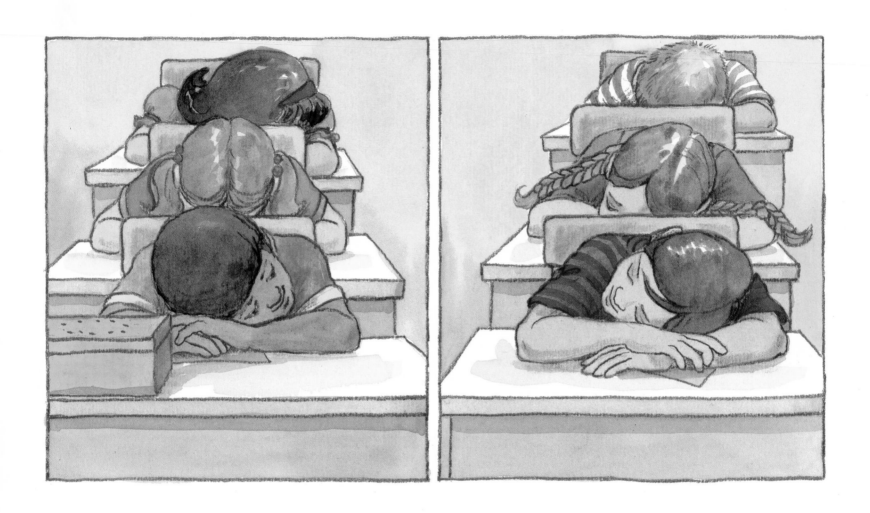

"This is ridiculous!" Mrs. Whitey said firmly. "Sit down and put your heads down! I'll count to three. One… two…three!"

"Now, I'm going on with the test. No more drinks. No
more bathroom. No more fooling around. We have eight more
words and not much time before gym. We'll have no more nonsense!"

Mrs. Whitey wasn't kidding.

It was so quiet you could hear the clock tick.

"All right," she began. "The next word is *new*."

Marlon's hand shot up.

"What is it now?" asked Mrs. Whitey.

"It's not fair," Marlon grumbled. "You're only supposed to give us words we studied."

"*New* isn't new," laughed Billy.

"That's right," said Mrs. Whitey. "*New* is old. Now write it."

"It?" asked Wendy.

"No, not *it*," said Mrs. Whitey. "Write the word that is the opposite of old."

"You mean young?" asked Angie.

"Wait. Which one?" asked Kevin. "New like a new pencil, or I knew the answer?"

"I never thought of that," laughed James.

"*New,*" said Mrs. Whitey, "like a new pair of shoes."

"Oh, oh, who's got an eraser?" yelled Marlon. "I wrote the wrong new."

"Forget the eraser," Mrs. Whitey said. "If you have a mistake, just cross it out."

"Mrs. Peloki doesn't let us," said Stephie.

"Yes, she does," Danny insisted. "She lets us have show-and-tell too."

"Honestly!" Mrs. Whitey said. "I'm sure you don't act this way when Mrs. Peloki is here."

"Marlon does," said Billy.

"So does he," Wendy said, pointing to Billy.

"Quiet!" said Mrs. Whitey. "Now this is a test and I
expect you to remember the rules." She wrote on the board:

1. No talking
2. Raise your hand if you have a question

"I have a question," said Marlon, raising his hand. "Why
can't we have show-and-tell? I want to know what's in
Danny's box."

"We'll have show-and-tell if we have time after
this test. Let's go on. Please write neatly."

"We never had that word," MariEllen said.

"What word?" asked Mrs. Whitey.

"Neatly," said Stephie. "It isn't on our list."

"I didn't ask you to spell neatly. I said to write neatly."

"I'm writing neatly," said Billy. "You want to see?"

"No, let's go on," said Mrs. Whitey. "The next word is…"

"You call that neat?" laughed James.

"Neat!" yelled Marlon. "Look at Danny's show-and-tell!"

"Enough!" said Mrs. Whitey.

"Enough? That's not on our list either," said MariEllen.

"I know," said Mrs. Whitey. "But there isn't enough time to finish this spelling test. It's time to line up for gym."

"All righty, Mrs. Whitey!" James shouted it and pretty soon everyone was saying it. "All righty, Mrs. Whitey!"

"But, Mrs. Whitey," said Danny. "We go home right after
gym, don't we? What about show-and-tell?"

"I've seen your *show*," said Mrs. Whitey, "and I'm going
to have to *tell* Mrs. Peloki to give you this test tomorrow."

Nobody seemed to remember that the next day was Saturday.